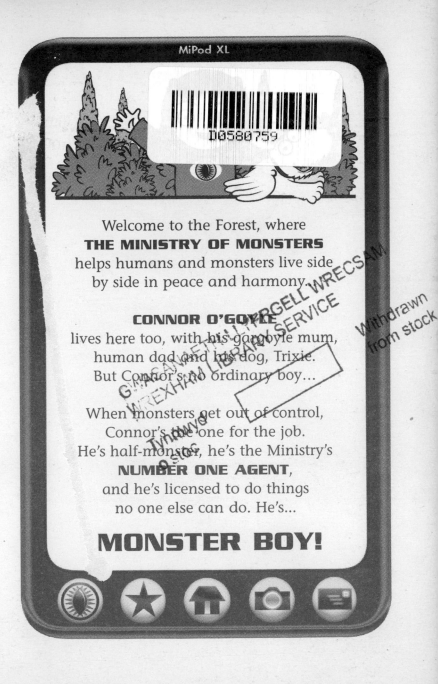

MiPod XL

Welcome to the Forest, where
THE MINISTRY OF MONSTERS
helps humans and monsters live side
by side in peace and harmony.

CONNOR O'GOYLE
lives here too, with his gargoyle mum,
human dad and his dog, Trixie.
But Connor's no ordinary boy...

When monsters get out of control,
Connor's the one for the job.
He's half-monster, he's the Ministry's
NUMBER ONE AGENT,
and he's licensed to do things
no one else can do. He's...

MONSTER BOY!

First published in 2009 by Orchard Books
First paperback publication in 2010

ORCHARD BOOKS
338 Euston Road, London NW1 3BH
Orchard Books Australia
Level 17/207 Kent St, Sydney, NSW 2000

ISBN 978 1 40830 247 7 (hardback)
ISBN 978 1 40830 255 2 (paperback)

1 3 5 7 9 10 8 6 4 2 (hardback)
1 3 5 7 9 10 8 6 4 2 (paperback)

Printed in Great Britain

Orchard Books is a division of Hachette Children's Books,
an Hachette UK company.

www.hachette.co.uk

MONSTER BOY

MINOTAUR MAZE

SHOO RAYNER

ORCHARD BOOKS

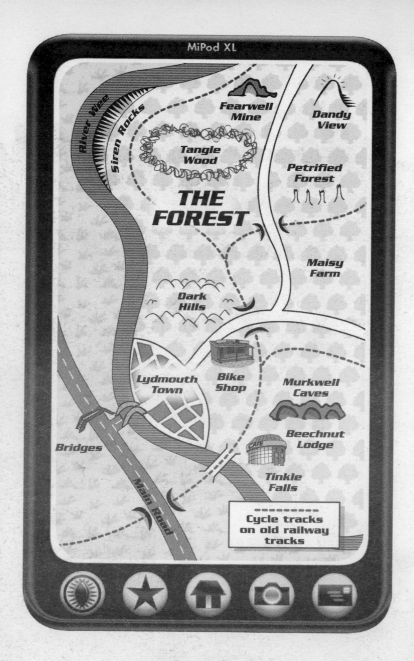

"This is your survival pack," Mum said, opening a hatch in the sleek body of MB5.

"That's so cool!" Connor grinned. "What's in it?"

Connor's mum had just finished building the new, top-secret, pedal-powered gyrocopter.

They were trying it out in one of Farmer Maisie's fields.

Mum showed Connor the contents of the waterproof container.

Inside was:

Top secret string for fishing or tying things up – it was long, strong and very light. Plus fishing hooks...

...a wind-up LED torch...

...an ultra-strong plastic sheet...

SURVIVAL PACK

...water-purifying pills for clean drinking water...

...and a miniature penknife, with a blade, scissors, file, pick and tweezers for removing thorns and splinters.

"And there's a fire-lighting kit – but you are only allowed to use it in real emergencies," said Mum sternly.

"Does this mean I have to catch fish if I get hungry?" Connor complained.

Mum popped open another hidden compartment and smiled. "You also have emergency sandwiches!"

"Woof!" barked Trixie, sniffing the hatch with interest.

"It's OK, Trixie," Mum laughed. "There's emergency dog food, too!"

Farmer Maisie was impressed with Mum's engineering skills.

"I wish you could invent something to bring people to my farm shop," she said. "I'll have to close it if we don't get some customers soon."

Just then, Connor's MiPod beeped.

MISSION ALERT!

To: Monster Boy,
Number One Agent

From: Mission Control,
Ministry of Monsters

Subject: Mino the Minotaur is
missing!

The Minotaur lives in Tangle Wood, near the old Fearwell coal mine. The waste rock from the mine makes excellent fertiliser so the trees and undergrowth are very thick. Mino might be trapped.

Please investigate immediately.
Good luck!

M.O.M.

THIS MESSAGE WILL SELF-ERASE IN FIFTEEN SECONDS

"Yeah!" whooped Connor. "Looks like a job for MB5. Let's see how well she flies. Come on, Trixie!"

Connor strapped on his helmet and pedalled hard across the grassy field.

The rotors swished above his head. The propeller buzzed behind his seat. In no time, the little craft lifted into the air. Connor laughed. Trixie yapped with joy as she flew alongside.

"Do be careful," Mum called after them. "Flying is not the same as riding a bike!"

"I'll be fine!" Connor yelled back.

Connor's mum was a Gargoyle, so
Connor was half-monster. His code-name
was Monster Boy. If anyone could look
after himself, Connor could.

Tangle Wood lived up to its name. Brushwood and brambles choked all the spaces between the trees. Connor pedalled and steered his gyrocopter over a sea of green.

From the air, Connor could see that a crazy pattern of paths had been slashed through the dense undergrowth.

Trixie barked and swooped down low. She had seen a large creature standing on the main path. When the creature saw Trixie, it ran away and disappeared into an old mine entrance.

Fearwell Mine 1872

"Come on, Trixie," Connor called to his dog. "Did you see his horns? I think that's the Minotaur. Let's go and have a closer look."

The main path was just wide and smooth enough to land on.

Connor typed a description of the creature into his MiPod to check what he was dealing with.

MiPOD MONSTER IDENTIFIER PROGRAM

Monster:

Minotaur

Distinguishing Features:
Minotaurs have the head of a bull and the body of a hairy ape-like man.

Preferred Habitat:
Dark caves and mazes.

Essential Information:
Some Minotaurs are especially fond of eating children and young people. They are not very good at reading maps or solving puzzles.

Danger Rating: 2

Connor tied his emergency fishing string onto the control-bar of MB5. "If we get lost in the dark, we can follow the string back here," he told Trixie.

The words "Fearwell Mine 1872" were carved into the rock above the mine entrance. A steel gate had been ripped off its hinges. A sign read, "Keep Out!"

Connor ignored it. He was allowed to go anywhere he needed to in the Forest.

Winding up the LED torch battery, Connor and Trixie entered the old, dark tunnel. Connor let out the fishing string behind him. Rotting wooden pit props held up the roof. Moisture trickled down the green, slimy walls.

The torchlight woke a family of bats.
They flapped their leathery wings
around Connor. Their high-pitched
squeaks drove Trixie wild with barking.

"Quiet, girl!"
Connor hissed.

Enormous spider webs clung to Connor's clothes as he and Trixie pushed further into the maze of tunnels. Pictures were painted onto the rock – pictures of giant bulls eating...people!

Without warning, the torchlight faded.
Connor fumbled in the dark. Trixie
growled. She sensed danger.

Connor found the wind-up handle on the torch and turned it furiously. The LEDs flickered, then sprang into life. Connor blinked.

Two huge eyes glowed red in his torch beam!

"Can I help you?" the
Minotaur bellowed.

"Wah!" Connor
dropped the torch and
let go of the string.

Connor's mind raced. If he ran, he would be lost for ever! What could he do?

"Please don't eat me!" Connor begged, in a thin, frightened voice.

"Eat you?" boomed the Minotaur. "Why would I want to eat you?"

"Don't Minotaurs eat people?" Connor asked.

"Not since we became vegetarians!"
the Minotaur answered in his gruff voice.
"We have very sensitive stomachs
actually," he explained. "People are
just too full of additives and junk food
these days."

Connor let out a sigh of relief. "I've been sent to look for you to see if you are all right," he explained.

"I'm fine," said the Minotaur. "But I'm stuck in Tangle Wood. I seem to be lost in my own maze!"

Trixie found the reel of string. She picked it up and dropped it at Connor's feet.

"Have you ever used string?" Connor asked. "Watch this."

Connor wound up the string as they made their way back through the maze of passages.

"That's really clever!" said the Minotaur, as they walked out into the sunshine. "I'd never get lost if I had some string like that."

Connor's MiPod beeped. It was a message from his dad, Gary O'Goyle, the world-famous Mountain Bike Champion. He always sent messages at the most unhelpful times!

Hi son,

Just won the Corn Cob Championship! We had to race through tall cornfields. It was like being in a maze! Got a great silver Corn Cob Trophy.

Lots of love,
Dad

"My dad's given me an idea!" Connor said. He gave the string to the Minotaur. "You can keep this," he explained. "Why don't you practise making paths with it? When you find your way out of Tangle Wood, I know someone who'd really like to meet you!"

A few weeks later, Connor and his mum cycled to Farmer Maisie's Farm Shop to buy some vegetables.

"What's going on?" asked Mum.
Parked cars lined the side of the road.
Families streamed through the farm
gates. A large sign announced:

Farmer Maisie's
Amazing Maize Maze!
Designed by
Mino the Minotaur

Children were having their photographs taken with the Minotaur. He'd become a bit of a celebrity.

Farmer Maisie looked happy. "Free tickets for you," she told Connor. "People love the Maize Maze and the farm shop is full of people."

Mino was happy, too. "Farmer Maisie pays me in yummy organic vegetables that are free from additives," he explained. "My stomach has never felt so good!"

Connor poked his mum in the ribs and ran into the tall field of maize. "Come on, Mum! Last one to the middle is a rotten old corn cob!"

TO THE MAZE

Trixie spread her wings wide and took to the air.

"Hey!" Connor called after her. "That's cheating!"

SHOO RAYNER
MONSTER BOY

Dino Destroyer	978 1 40830 248 4
Mummy Menace	978 1 40830 249 1
Dragon Danger	978 1 40830 250 7
Werewolf Wail	978 1 40830 251 4
Gorgon Gaze	978 1 40830 252 1
Ogre Outrage	978 1 40830 253 8
Siren Spell	978 1 40830 254 5
Minotaur Maze	978 1 40830 255 2

All priced at £3.99

The Monster Boy stories are available from all good bookshops,
or can be ordered direct from the publisher:
Orchard Books, PO BOX 29, Douglas IM99 1BQ
Credit card orders please telephone 01624 836000
or fax 01624 837033 or visit our website: www.orchardbooks.co.uk
or e-mail: bookshop@enterprise.net for details.

To order please quote title, author and ISBN
and your full name and address.
Cheques and postal orders should be made payable to 'Bookpost plc.'
Postage and packing is FREE within the UK
(overseas customers should add £2.00 per book).

Prices and availability are subject to change.